Dick and Jane
Hide-and-Seek

By Kristin Ostby
Illustrated by Larry Ruppert

Grosset & Dunlap

GROSSET & DUNLAP
Published by the Penguin Group
Penguin Group (USA) Inc., 375 Hudson Street, New York, New York 10014, U.S.A.
Penguin Group (Canada), 90 Eglinton Avenue East, Suite 700, Toronto, Ontario, Canada M4P 2Y3
(a division of Pearson Penguin Canada Inc.)
Penguin Books Ltd, 80 Strand, London WC2R 0RL, England
Penguin Ireland, 25 St Stephen's Green, Dublin 2, Ireland
(a division of Penguin Books Ltd)
Penguin Group (Australia), 250 Camberwell Road, Camberwell, Victoria 3124, Australia
(a division of Pearson Australia Group Pty Ltd)
Penguin Books India Pvt Ltd, 11 Community Centre, Panchsheel Park, New Delhi - 110 017, India
Penguin Group (NZ), Cnr Airborne and Rosedale Roads, Albany, Auckland 1310, New Zealand
(a division of Pearson New Zealand Ltd)
Penguin Books (South Africa) (Pty) Ltd, 24 Sturdee Avenue, Rosebank, Johannesburg 2196, South Africa

Penguin Books Ltd, Registered Offices:
80 Strand, London WC2R 0RL, England

Dick and Jane™ is a trademark of Pearson Education, Inc. Text and illustrations copyright © 2007 by
Pearson Education, Inc. All rights reserved. Published by Grosset & Dunlap, a division of Penguin Young Readers Group,
345 Hudson Street, New York, New York 10014. GROSSET & DUNLAP is a trademark of Penguin Group (USA) Inc. Printed in the U.S.A.

Library of Congress Control Number: 2006016584

ISBN 978-0-448-44467-3   10 9 8 7 6 5 4 3 2

Dick and Jane and Sally want to play.
They want to play hide-and-seek.
Who will be it?

"Not it!" says Dick.
"Not it!" says Sally.
"I will be it," says Jane.

Jane covers her eyes.
She counts to twenty.
Dick and Sally run and hide.
"Ready or not, here I come!" says Jane.

Jane looks for Dick and Sally.
Something is behind the plant.
Is it Dick?
Is it Sally?

No, it is not Dick or Sally.
It is Spot!
Spot is playing with his ball.
Silly, silly Spot.

Jane looks in Sally's room.
There is a bump in Sally's bed.
"Sally, is that you?" asks Jane.

No, it is not Sally.
It is Sally's teddy bear!

Jane walks into the kitchen.
Something is under thc kitchen table.
"Dick, is that you?" asks Jane.

No, it is not Dick.
It is Puff!
Puff is sleeping.
"You are not Dick!" Jane laughs.

Jane looks into the bathroom.
There is a shadow behind the shower curtain.
The shadow looks like Dick!
"Dick, is that you?" asks Jane.

"You found me!" says Dick.
"I was hiding in the shower.
Now we will go find Sally.
We will go find Sally together."

"Where could Sally be?" asks Dick.
"Where could Sally be?" asks Jane.

"Sally is not behind the plant," says Jane.
"Sally is not in her bedroom.
  She is not under the kitchen table.
  She is not in the shower."

"Maybe Sally is in the closet," says Dick.
Is Sally in the closet?
Is Sally there?

"Look, Dick," says Jane.
"Sally is not in the closet.
 There are only clothes in the closet.
 And coats and hats, too."

Dick and Jane wear coats and hats.
They are playing detective!
What is that sound at the window?
Is Sally behind the curtain?

"Look, Jane," says Dick.
"Sally is not behind the curtain.
  Mother is outside watering flowers."

"Hello, Dick! Hello, Jane!" Mother says.
"Hello, Mother!" Dick and Jane say.

"Father," says Jane.
"Oh, Father, can you help?" she asks.
"We cannot find Sally.
  Have you seen Sally?"

"I have not seen Sally," Father says.
"But I saw somebody." Father winks.
"Somebody went into Dick's bedroom."

Dick and Jane look in Dick's bedroom.
Where is Sally?
Where could little Sally be?
There is something underneath Dick's bed.
"Sally, is that you?" asks Dick.

It is Sally!
Sally is hiding there!
Funny little Sally.
There you are!

"I hid under the bed!" says Sally.
"I hid, and you could not find me!"
Sally is very clever.
Clever, clever Sally!

What a fun game of hide-and-seek!
What fun it is to play together.
Dick and Jane and Sally have so much fun!